pyjama-rama

The Sleep-over Handbook

Caroline Clayton

Bloomsbury

Acknowledgements

Thanks to Emily and Matilda, and Hannah,
David, Jesse, Niall, Mark, Kate, James D.,
Antronella, Amy, Taeo, Lawrence and Kiri
at Hanover School, North London.

Thanks also to
Tina Stevens and Mike Clowes.

Contents

ONE

Let's Party!

There's nothing better than a good girlie night in with your closest buddies . . . apart from a slumber party of course, when the fun carries on until morning.

Slumber parties, also known as sleep-overs and pyjama parties, are more fun than your common-or-garden get-togethers because:

- You never have to leave just as you're getting in the swing of things.

- You don't have to pester Mum and Dad to pick you up before bedtime.

- You get to stay up a lot later than normal.

- You can keep talking late into the night, long after lights-out.

- You get a few hours of extra fun the next morning.

You don't really need an excuse for throwing a slumber party, but just in case, here are ten of the best:

1 It's your birthday.

2 It's Friday and school's out tomorrow.

3 You've got a new duvet and pillowcase set.

4 You want to watch *Grease* on video for the millionth time.

5 It's your turn to invite a friend back to your place.

6 Your room is tidy for once!

7 The nights are drawing in.

8 You fancy a pillow fight.

9 You need someone to help you crunch your way through a big bag of DIY popcorn.

10 There's an 'R' in the month!

The truth is that anytime is a good time to throw a slumber party. But don't even think about hosting your own sleep-over until you've read this book.

It's full of helpful hints about how to have a lorra lorra larks with your chums – *the essential guide to making a slumber party really rumba!*

Behind every great slumber party there's a hostess who's done her homework. A little preparation, dedication, motivation and inspiration can make the difference between having a good party and having a really brilliant one. If you want to be the hostess with the mostest and make your party a real pyjamarama . . . read on!

TWO:

Getting Ready

You've decided to host your own sleep-over. So what happens next? You've got to plan the theme for your party – that's what!

Throwing a themed party is a good idea because it immediately gives your party a focus. A theme will get your friends involved straight away – anyone who has to make an extra effort before they turn up is much less likely to be a party pooper on the night. You could even fire up your friends by letting them help you choose the theme. Here are a few suggestions:

Clocks-go-back Party

A wonderful way to celebrate the onset of wintery nights. And you're guaranteed an extra hour of fun.

Halloween

Start off the evening with some trick or treating. Then spook yourselves silly telling ghostly stories after lights out!

A Pink Pyjama Party

Everyone comes dressed in pink, pink, and nothing but pink! Serve pink drinks (strawberry milkshakes or cranberry juice) and pink snacks (prawn cocktail flavoured crisps, pink meringues and strawberries dunked in melted white chocolate). Yummy!

Bring-a-present Party

Set a limit on how much everyone should spend (somewhere between, say 50p and £2.50). Put all the gifts into a box and take it in turns to pick one out. (Make sure no one ends up with the pressie they brought with them, though!)

Clothes-swop Party

The idea is that everyone turns up with gear they've outgrown or simply grown tired of. Then everyone takes turns holding up their goodies and hands them over to whoever wants them most. Keep an eye out for anyone getting more than their fair share, and make sure nobody goes home empty handed.

Karaoke Party

No need to hire a fancy bit of kit, as long as you've got a tape player you're away and warbling. Who needs a microphone anyway?

Fifties Party

Put your hair in a ponytail and croon around in your bobbysox, *Grease*-style.

Popstar Party

Ask your pals to come dressed up as a famous pop star. Later on, get everyone to do a star turn and video them for posterity. Give a prize for the best effort.

Make-up Party

Ask your chums to come clutching their make-up bags. Then you can chuck all your combined cosmetics into one big box and have fun trying out a totally different look.

Hair-style Party

Spend the evening styling
one another's hair
(see Chapter 9).

Party Invites

Handing out party invitations is more fun and much cheaper than summoning your soul sisters by phone. Watch your mates' faces as you plonk one in their hand. Receiving their replies is even more of a thrill. Have fun making your own design. Because you're having a sleep-over, why not style the invitations in the shape of:

a night cap

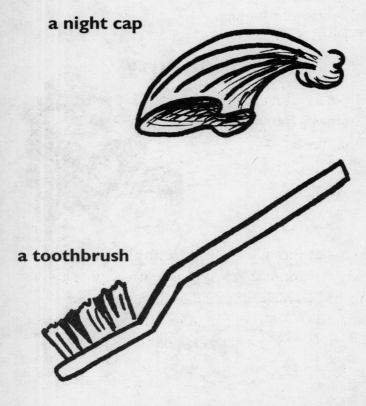

a toothbrush

a pair of slippers

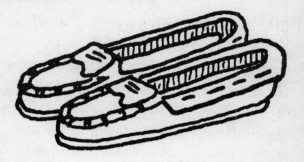

a sleeping bag?

Try to make the invites tie-in with the theme of the party (if there is one). Make sure you ask your pals to RSVP (répondez s'il vous plaît – that means 'reply' in French). After all you'll need to know how many guests to expect for brekkie.

Plan Your Party

What do you do once you've decided on a theme for the party, made and mailed out your invitations? The next thing you need is a party planner.

The rest of this book contains zillions of cool ideas on ways to make your party go with a swing. Then, once you've decided what you're going to do, you should work out a timetable for when you're going to do it. Here's an example:

4 p.m. Everyone arrives.

4.30 Treasure Hunt, followed by a few fun games, followed by some magic tricks (see chapter 7).

6 p.m. Teatime.

6.45 Video viewing.

8 p.m. Everyone into their PJs!

8.15 Retire to the bedroom for a round of "Truth or Dare" and some serious pillow talk (see chapter 8).

10.30	Lights out!
11.00	Force yourself to stay awake by playing word games.
12.00	Midnight Feast.

Make your own party planner, and don't forget to include:

Now, are you ready for the fun to start? No way, José! You haven't even tidied your room yet!

THREE

The Little Things

Once you've made your plans and tidied your room, what's next on the agenda? Well, now is the time to pay attention to the details. It's the little things that matter, whether you're hosting a party or are going to be a guest. Here, for your information, is the ultra-cool guide to doing the right thing!

Get some cool kit. Sporting the right kind of togs for bed is crucial. How do you know what's sizzling and what, frankly, has gone rather flat?

in

Big baggy T-shirts worn with boxer shorts or a pair of comfy leggings

Glitter slouch socks

Pocohontas-style moccasin slippers

Towelling dressing-gown in creamy-pastel colours

Toothbrushes that change colour

Endangered animals wash-bags and soaps

☼Out

Slippers with big fluffy pompons

Tartan booties (the kind Granny wears to warm her tootsies)

Frilly Victorian-style nighties

Night caps

Using a plastic carrier bag as a wash bag

It's important not to take sleep-over style too seriously. Remember that fashion is about fun, not friction. Treat the whole fashion scene as a game, and you'll have a good time.

You can even turn style-wars into a fun game at bedtime by rating one another's slumber gear. Award each other points for cool clothes. Deduct points for really naff items. Here are a few suggestions to get you started, though you can make up your own scoring system as you go along.

+10 points for a Hunchback of Notre Dame/ Flipper night shirt
-15 for anything with My Little Pony/ Barbie on it!
+5 points for anything pink
+10 points for anything purple
+10 points for anything stripey

+15 points for anything that changes colour
+20 points for anything that glows in the dark
+2 points for anything with Mickey and Minnie on it
-2 points for anything with Polly Pocket on it
+50 points for anything with a Dr Martens logo on it

Lingo

Before your guests arrive, ask yourself if you're speaking their language? Just about the worst gaff you can make is to start jabbering in the kind of lingo that went out yonks ago.

IN	OUT
Mad	Mental
Wicked	Brill
Full-on	Mega
Sweet	Trendy
Cool	Stonking
Top	Funky
Funksome	Bonkers
Rock'n'roll	Britpop
Chick	Babe
Crucial	Essential

All right? Now you're well on your way to a totally, full-on, wicked pyjamarama your mates will be mad for!

Vital Videos

Chilling out with a video is part and parcel of a cosy slumber party. But it's important to chose a corker. Here are ten of the best:

Free Willy/Free Willy II
A whale of a movie with a fin-tastic follow up. They're splashing!

Grease
Pyjama party fifties' style – altogether now, 'Well-a, well-a, well-a, ooh, tell me more, tell me more . . .'

The Secret Garden
A gloriously magical movie based on Frances Hodgson Burnett's brilliant book.

A Little Princess
Erm, another gloriously magical movie based on another brilliant book by erm, Frances Hodgson Burnett.

Pocahontas
Disney's original all-American supermodel lookie-likey!

Mrs Doubtfire
A naughty nineties Mary Poppins

Adams Family Values
They're kookie and they're crazy . . . and they
really make the most of summer camp!

*Ace Ventura: Pet Detective/Ace Ventura:
When Nature Calls*
He's Ace and he's quite hilarious too!

The Nightmare Before Christmas
Perfect for Halloween – it'll scare your socks off!

Magic Eye Videos
These contain dozens of 3-D images but not everyone gets them. Turn your viewing into a game, and
give a prize for the player to see each one first.

FOUR

No Parents Allowed

Parents. Where would we be without them, eh? Well, probably not born actually, but then again, if we didn't have lovely Mum or Dad around we'd have no one to complain about or be embarrassed by.

Although parents complain a lot, they're not very easily embarrassed. When you were a baby they positively adored it when you covered them in dribbly sick or pooed on their hands while they tried to change your nappy. You see, part of being a parent is growing a skin as thick as rhino hide. You'll *never* manage to embarrass your mum or dad. And these days they take pleasure in embarrassing YOU!

In fact, parents are fine most of the time, but when your mates appear, their chorus of cringe-making comments commences. Parents love embarrassing you in front of your friends and then pretending they haven't a clue they've done anything wrong.

Here's some typical blush-making parent-babble:

"So and so was such a fat baby."
(They're talking about YOU!)

"How's that boil on your bum? Does it need lancing?"

Anthing that starts with: "When I was your age . . ."

"Play that lovely tune on your recorder for Auntie Mabel."

Once you invite your pals over to party with you, you put yourself at risk. Your parents could blow your cool. Any one of the above comments could slip from their mouths at any moment!

The only way to deal
with embarrassing
parents is to keep
them separate from
your friends – and
that rule applies to
naughty brothers and
sisters too! If you
haven't got a lock on
 your bedroom door
(and most parents are
too canny to allow one!)
you'll need to keep them out with a
'Do Not Disturb' notice.

You should also invent a whole load of excuses
to stop them from straying into your room.
This might be particularly hard once they
hear you enjoying yourselves. You can bet that
while you're jumping off the beds and grooving
to Take That's *Greatest Hits*, they'll be downstairs
worrying that the ceiling is going to cave in.

If your wardrobe topples over and your
parents bellow, 'What's going on in there?', do
not under any circumstances reply, 'Nothing!'.
This will make them crash your room faster
than a cheetah on roller skates. Instead, keep
them calm . . .

By saying you're . . .	**When what you're really doing is . . .**
just having a nice game of Barbie dolls.	giving Barbie a mohican haircut.
learning a new language.	learning to rap like Coolio.
pouring over a bit of local history.	telling your mates how old your parents are.
sorting out your cupboards.	emptying the entire contents of your cupboards onto your bedroom floor.
experimenting with make-up.	experimenting with Mum's most expensive make-up!

More Excuses that Might Come in Handy

The party's in full swing, and you're making more noise than a footie crowd. Mum or Dad comes storming into the room and says:

"Didn't you hear me shouting?"

You can say: **"No, actually we were making a lot of noise ourselves!"**

It's way past midnight and you and your mate(s) still can't stop giggling. Mum or Dad demands: **"Why aren't you asleep yet?"**

You can say: **"We're doing our night class homework – we're learning to read in the dark!"**

It's past midnight and that salted popcorn has left you with a wicked thirst. Mum and Dad will soon want to know why you need another glass of water.

You can say: **"The bedrooms on fire!"**
(NB: Remember to tell them that this is a JOKE, if you would like any more pocket-money before you take your GCSEs that is!)

If you can't manage to send your parents to another planet for the evening, you'll have to do your best to keep them sweet. Why not hire the entire series of *Pride and Prejudice* from the video shop. That'll have them glued to their seats and they simply won't notice any naughtiness going on – even if it is happening right under their noses!

FIVE

How to be the Perfect Hostess

When you invite your pals around to stop over at your place you suddenly become responsible for giving them a good time. If the thought of keeping your friends happy and contented for over half a day sounds rather scary, fret not!

Making sure your friends have a fun-filled time needn't turn you into a stress puppy – in fact, playing the perfect hostess can be quite a hoot provided you prepare your family and your guests for the party. When families and friends mix there's usually plenty of opportunity for things to go wrong. Your role is to try to stop anything embarrassing from happening. That means alerting your guests to things that might strike them as strange even though they don't seem at all odd to you.

You see, staying at somebody else's house can be a bit like visiting a foreign country – people do things differently there. Every family has their own peculiar habits but, as the saying goes, 'forewarned is forearmed'. For example, warn your friends of any of these problems:

If your central heating makes spooky
rumbling noises in the night.

If your toilet requires
a fancy flushing
technique.

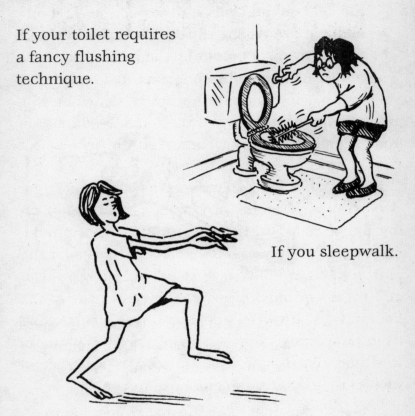

If you sleepwalk.

If your parents set the burglar alarm
during the night.

(You'll need to explain which parts of the house
are night-time no-go zones. You don't want your
pal wandering around the house setting it off by
accident, do you?)

A Good Host Always...

★ Finds out whether her guest likes to sleep with
the light on (and will, if necessary, leave it on
all night even if she usually sleeps in the dark).

★ Leaves a box of tissues by the bed for those
homesick and blubsome moments.

★ Warns her parents not to ask a friend any (repeat
ANY) direct questions. If possible, all enquiries
and comments must come through you!

★ Always, always puts parents under strict
instructions not to kiss friend(s) goodnight.
Watching an over-friendly mum or dad pucker-
ing up towards a nervous pal is cringe-making
enough. But witnessing the sorry sight of the
same pal desperately ducking for safety
beneath the duvet can make your toes curl!
Remember, parents and pals are best kept apart.

A Good Host Never...

* Sniggers at a guest's teddy bear or comforter - it's impolite!
* Embarrasses a mate by repeating any daft mumblings she made in her sleep.
* Knowingly starts snoozing when a friend is in mid-sentence.

One other thing . . . If it's the first time you've invited a particular pal over, her parents may be a bit nervous about letting her stay. After all, they've no way of knowing that your parents won't be jetting off on a two-week trip to Timbuktu the moment their darling daughter checks in. Reassure them by getting Mum or Dad to phone up and let them know that you've no plans to re-enact *Home Alone* and that there will be a responsible adult supervising your fun!

Are You a Good Hostess?

Check out how far you'd go to put your guests' feelings first.

---

1) **Do you expect your guests to turn up at your parties with pressies for you?**
a) Of course!
b) Of course not! You're just pleased they could make it.
c) No, but if they did you'd be as pleased as punch.

---

2) **It's bedtime and your best mate has suddenly gone a bit misty-eyed and looks rather homesick. Do you:**
a) give her a cuddle and lend her your favourite teddy to snuggle up with?
b) suggest she phones her mum and dad to say goodnight?
c) ignore it. After all, you don't want to start off a full-blown blubbering session do you?

---

3) **Would you describe yourself as:**
a) a listener?
b) a talker?
c) a bit of both?

4) You like sleeping with the light on but you suspect your friend prefers the dark. Do you:

a) switch off your light and hope your mate doesn't hear you trembling under your duvet . . . its only for eight hours, after all!

b) introduce her to the pleasures of 60-watt sleep? Kipping in the dark is just too scary to think about!

c) pin in one of those cutesy animal night-light plugs next to your bed instead? Its reassuring glow will keep you happy but won't keep her awake.

5) Which of these is the most important thing a good hostess can do?

a) Warn a guest if the bathroom lock is broken.

b) Splash out on a load of extras to make bath time more fun (for example, bath oils and bubble bath).

c) Involve your friend in making as many decisions as possible about the fun you'll be having, for example, let her choose what video to watch.

6) Who's your idea of the perfect host?

a) Anthea Turner?

b) Chris Evans?

c) Basil Fawlty?

---

7) You both wake up early next morning before the rest of the house shows any signs of movement. Do you:

a) persuade your pal to fetch you a cup of tea? You can't function in the morning without one!

b) get up and bring your friend breakfast in bed?

c) start scoffing that midnight feast you were too tired to eat last night?

Scores

1) a 1, b 3, c 2   2) a 3, b 2, c 1   3) a 2, b 1, c 3   4) a 3, b 1, c 2   5) a 2, b 1, c 3   6) a 3, b 2, c 5!   7) a 1, b 3, c 2

So, How do you Rate as a Good Host?

15–21: You're the hostess with the mostest. You know that when you've got a friend over you have to put her wishes before your own. But that doesn't mean you moan about the sacrifices you've had to make or become a real bossy boots. You know what having fun with friends is about – give and take.

10–14: You're a good host – not too pushy and over the top which might make some friends feel slightly uncomfortable. You avoid your guest getting flustered or embarrassed at all costs.

9 or under: You're not exactly the perfect hostess because you tend to put your own needs first. Hosting a party is really about looking after your friends, putting their wishes first and making sure that they have a good time. More effort needed in the future.

SIX

How to be the Perfect Guest

Being a good guest isn't just about being well-behaved and polite. It's about relaxing, laughing and really enjoying yourself.

Remember that, as a guest, your mood could make or break the party atmosphere. If you don't feel up to staying over at a pal's house even though you've already said you'll go, don't be afraid to pull out. It's better to turn down the invitation than turn up looking like a wet weekend in Bognor, especially if there are going to be quite a few people staying over. If you act all gloomy you could end up spoiling everybody's fun. And you'll be branded a real party pooper!

Of course, everyone gets nervous before a party, but these pre-party nerves actually add to the excitment and your enjoyment of the evening. If you'd like to sleep over at a friend's house but have any worries about it, talk about your fears to your mum or dad. If you go through with the invitation, explain to your host that you sometimes get scared staying away from home but that you're hoping it will be OK. A good host will make an extra effort to look after you.

Don't be a Party Pooper

- ★ Don't squeeze your host's toothpaste from the middle of the tube.
- ★ Don't leave the top off the toothpaste.
- ★ Don't laugh if you find out your host still sleeps with a teddy!
- ★ Don't boss your friend around on her home territory.

Six Ways to Win Your Hostess's Heart

♥ Find out whether you need to bring your own duvet or a sleeping bag with you.

♥ Be cheery – even if you're feeling a teensy bit homesick.

♥ Let your friend know whether you'll be wanting the light on before you go to bed.

❤ Give your mate's mum plenty of warning if you really can't abide Brussels sprouts or spam fritters – then you won't see them wobbling on that plate in front of you at teatime!

❤ Resist the temptation to call Mum and Dad to pick you up. Everyone feels homesick from time to time and that feeling of sadness will soon wear off, if you let it. Chances are you'll soon have yourself so much fun you'll forget about it.

❤ Warn your hostess if you sleep walk!

Are You the Perfect Guest?

Being a perfect guest is as important as being a great host. Just how good a guest are you? Try our quiz and find out.

1) **It's bedtime and you're starting to feel an itsy bit homesick. Do you:**
a) suddenly sob your heart out and demand to be taken home?
b) try to put the feeling out of your mind, and hope it soon passes?
c) throw yourself into enjoying the party, and suddenly remember that you're not feeling homesick any more?

2) **You accidentally spill your bedtime drink in bed. Do you:**
a) come clean and have a giggle clearing the mess up?
b) keep quiet and hope that blackcurrent and banana milk shakes won't stain the sheets?
c) start crying and insist that your friend's mum puts new sheets on the bed?

3) It's video time. You're friend wants to watch *Grease* but you'd rather watch something you haven't seen before. Do you:

a) let her decide, after all, she took the trouble of renting them from the video hire shop?

b) feel quite strongly that as the guest you should have the casting vote?

c) avoid an argument by suggesting you do something else instead, such as a bit of hair braiding?

4) Would you describe yourself as:

a) a listener?

b) a talker?

c) a bit of both?

5) Who's your idea of the perfect host?
a) Anthea Turner?
b) Zoë Ball?
c) Victor Meldrew?

6) You've had a great time at a pal's sleep-over. Do you:
a) call home and beg to be allowed to stay another night?
b) pop back to her place a few days later with a huge box of chocs and your toothbrush – just in case?

c) write a thank-you note and plan a return party round at your place?

Score
1) a 1, b 2, c 3 2) a 2, b 1, c 3 3) a 3, b 1, c 2
4) a 2, b 1, c 3 5) a 3, b 2, c –10! 6) a 1, b 2, c 3

So, How do You Rate as a Good Guest?

13–18: It's official! You're a great guest (and fun friend) to have around! You're a proper pal who's thoughtful about your host and other people.

8–12: You're a good guest, who knows that being a brat when you're playing away can be a risky business, so you take pains to please your host. Remember, though, that being a cool friend is about giving as well as taking. Invite your friends back to your place more if you want to stay on the scene.

8 and under: Not even Lumiere and Cogsworth would want you to be their guest again in a hurry! Perhaps you're a little too timid, which can spoil everyone else's fun as well as your own. Or perhaps you expect to be waited on hand and foot just because you're not at home. Whichever, you need to wise up and work on becoming a good guest.

SEVEN

Funtastic Feasts

Isn't it funny how food plays such a huge part in party preparations? Or rather, worrying about food plays a huge part in party preparations. Part and parcel of hosting any party is making sure your guests don't go hungry.

Lots of hosts panic once they've invited a friend round. They think they've got to keep her tummy topped up for the whole time of the stay. In fact, you don't have to feed your guests *all* the time, though inviting friends to sleep over does mean you'll have to lay on at least two main meals: tea or supper and breakfast, not to mention munchies for a midnight feast!

Cooking tea should come top of your priorities. Depending on how many people you've invited round, you could always rope them into the cooking. Getting creative in the kitchen can be marvellous fun too – but remember, if you're using the oven or hob, make sure an adult helps.

Plan your main meal a few days before the party. Find out:

- about your friends' favourite scoff;

- whether any guests are veggies;

- if anyone is allergic to any nosh (e.g. nuts);

- what kind of foods would fit in with the theme of your party (if you've chosen one)?

To get you going, this chapter contains loads of recipe ideas. Each one will serve four friends.

❧ Heart-shaped Sandwiches ❧

You'll need:
24 thin slices of soft, white bread
a heart-shaped cutter
butter
a 200g tin of pink salmon
a tube of cheese spread

1   Cut 24 heart shapes from the sliced bread.
    (If you position the cutter carefully you should
    be able to get two hearts per slice.)

2   Spread each heart with butter.

3   Cover each heart with finely-mashed pink
    salmon or cheese spread.

Hot Dogs

You'll need:
16 chipolata sausages
16 long, soft, hot-dog rolls
butter
ketchup, relish or mustard

1 Grill the sausages.

2 Split the rolls lengthways, leaving a 'hinge' and butter them.

3 Slot a sausage into each roll and serve with sweetcorn relish, tomato ketchup or mustard.

Pyjama Party Pizzas

You'll need:
8 wholemeal muffins (or mini pizza bases)
4 tablespoons of tomato pizza topping
25g mozzarella cheese
toppings:
black olives, a sliced courgette, diced green and red
peppers, sliced mushroom, fresh chopped parsley,
diced ham, anchovies, pineapple chunks

1   Preheat the oven to 200° C/400° F/Gas mark 6.

2   Cut the cheese into
    very thin slices.

3   Slice each muffin in half. Then
    spread two tablespoons of the
    tomato sauce on the cut
    side of the muffin (or
    on each pizza base
    if you're using
    them instead).

4 Add a little cheese to each muffin, plus any of the toppings suggested above that tickle your taste buds.

5 Put in the oven for 15–20 minutes.

Veggie Burgers

You'll need:

450g mashed, boiled potato

one egg

75g grated cheddar cheese

150g frozen mixed vegetables

10g sunflower seeds

one tablespoon of fresh parsley, chopped

2 spring onions, chopped

25g fresh wholemeal breadcrumbs

2 tablespons of olive oil

salt and pepper

1   Thaw out the frozen veg. Then pop them
    in a big bowl with the potato, egg, cheese,
    sunflower seeds, onions, parsley and
    breadcrumbs. Beat together well.

2   Leave in the fridge for 20 mins to cool.

3   Turn the mixture onto a table top and shape
    into 8 burgers.

4   Heat the oil in a large frying pan and fry
    each burger for 1-2 minutes on each side
    until golden brown.

5   Serve the burgers hot with beans and coleslaw.

Club Sandwiches

They're a double-decker delight!

You'll need:

a white sandwich loaf of bread, cut into 16 medium-thick slices, lightly toasted and spread with butter
4 eggs, hard boiled and sliced
4 slices of cooked turkey or chicken
4 slices of cheese
2 sliced tomatoes
mayonnaise
a handful of cress
salt and pepper

1   Take one slice of buttered bread and cover with egg and cress.

2   Sprinkle with salt and pepper and top with another slice of bread.

3   Then cover with a slice of turkey or chicken and dab with a spoonful of mayonnaise.

4   Cover with another slice of bread. Then layer on a slice of cheese and a few slices of tomato. Season with salt and pepper.

5   Finish off with a final slice of bread. Then cut the club sandwich into four triangles. Skewer each triangle with a cocktail stick for that ultra-professional look.

Once you've eaten your main course, you'll also want
to try some perfect puds.

Fried Banana Delight

You'll need:
6 under-ripe bananas
3 tablespoons of water
450g sugar

1 Slice the bananas.

2 Dissolve the sugar in the water in a large
frying pan, over a low heat.

3 Turn up the heat and bring to the boil.
Bubble until the syrup is a golden brown
colour (called caramel).

4 Lay the bananas in the caramel and spoon it
over them until they are coated.

5 Fry for about 5 minutes. Then serve with
a little caramel poured over them.

Banana Choc Buns

You'll need:
225g self-raising flour
100g soft butter
25g plain chocolate drops
25g white chocolate drops
3oz raisins
one under-ripe banana, chopped
one egg, beaten
one or two tablespoons of milk
a little demerara sugar, for sprinkling

1 Preheat your oven to 200° C/400° F/Gas mark 6 and lightly grease a baking tray for when your buns are ready.

2 Rub the butter into the flour until the mixture looks like fine breadcrumbs.

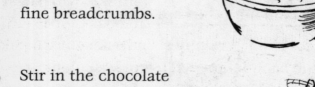

3 Stir in the chocolate drops, raisins and banana.

4 Add the egg and
   enough milk to
   make a stiff mixture,
   taking care that it's
   not too dry.

5 Spoon the mixture into little
   heaps on the baking tray,
   leaving space between
   each one.

6

Sprinkle with sugar
and bake for 10–15
minutes until a pale
golden colour.

Chocolate Crispies

They're a classic!

You'll need:
25g butter
25g icing sugar
one tablespoon
of golden syrup
25g cocoa powder
25g cornflakes or rice
crispies (depending on
which you like best)
paper bun cases

1 Melt the butter and syrup in a pan over a low heat.

2 Stir in the icing sugar.

3 Add the cocoa powder and stir until the mixture is smooth.

4 Stir in the cornflakes/crispies a handful at a time until they are completely but not heavily covered in the choccy mixture. You might want to keep adding a few more handfuls until the coating looks just right.

5 Spoon the mixture into the bun cases and leave to cool.

Mint Choc-chip ice-cream

You'll need:
300ml double cream
175ml can of condensed milk
$1^1/_2$ teaspoons of peppermint essence
a few drops of green food colouring
100g chocolate chips

1   Pour the cream and condensed milk into a
    large mixing bowl.

2   Add the peppermint essence and use an electric
    whisk to whip up the mixture until it is thick and
    forms soft peaks.

3   Stir in the green food colouring and chocolate chips.

4   Scrape the mixture into an old ice-cream
    container and put on the lid.

5   Place in the freezer for 3–4 hours until firm.
    Then enjoy!

Top Tip
You can make your own
chocolate chips by putting a
chocolate bar inside a plastic bag
and bashing it with
a rolling pin.

Butterscotch
Brilliant with ice-cream!

You'll need:
75g unsalted butter
450g granulated sugar
one tablespoon of lemon juice
a few drops of lemon essence

1   Melt the butter in a saucepan on a low heat.

2   Add the sugar and stir until it has melted.
    Then turn up the heat and let it boil, stirring
    all the time.

3   Add the lemon juice and keep stirring the mix-
    ture until it turns light brown and becomes
    brittle. You can test whether it is brittle by
    dropping a little into a cup of cold water. If it
    goes hard, it's ready!

4   Add a few drops of lemon essence, stir well and
    pour into an oiled toffee tin to about 5mm deep.

5   When the butterscotch is nearly cool, cut into
    oblong pieces and leave until it is completely
    cold and hard.

Besides food, you'll also need some delicious drinks.

Milk Shakes

For each shake you'll need:
300 ml milk
one generous spoonful of ice-cream
one teaspoon of milkshake flavouring syrup

1   Put all the ingredients in an electric blender
    and whisk until frothy. If you don't have a
    blender, put the ingredients in a jug and whisk
    hard.

2   Serve immediately with a straw.

Coke Floats

Pour a glass of ice-cold cola. Then float a scoop of
vanilla ice-cream on the top. Drink it while it's a-
fizzing! Americans calls this a Brown Cow!

Natural Fruit Shakes

For each shake you'll need:
300 ml milk
one generous spoonful of ice-cream
soft fruit (e.g. half a banana, a handful of strawberries)

1 Sieve or blend the fruit to a pulp.

2 Add the pulped fruit to the milk and ice-cream and blend or whisk until frothy.

3 Serve immediately with a straw.

Midnight Feasts

Sleep-overs and midnight feasts go together like jelly and ice-cream. And what's more, they're one of the few occasions when Mum or Dad might turn a blind eye to a coating of crumbs on your bedroom carpet.

Obviously if you've eaten tea earlier in the evening you're not going to feel like a four-course meal when the clock strikes midnight. But there's bound to be room in your tums for a few late-night snacks or a couple of cold pizzas and other supper left-overs.

For a magic midnight feast, just follow these simple ten dos and don'ts:

✴ Don't snack the entire evening – leave a little room in your tum for the food to come.

✴ Don't let your brother(s) or sister(s) see you sneaking food up the stairs. The last thing you want is for your feast to be crashed by dribbling siblings.

✴ Don't plan to get a few hours kip in before the feast. If you set your alarm clock to wake you, your whole family might turn up too.

* Do play pillow games to keep you awake until it's time to scoff.

* Do keep the feast a secret if your parents don't approve of snacking out when you should be crashing out!

* Don't munch on crisps or other things that really go CRUNCH in the night!

* Don't bother with drinks unless you have an ensuite bathroom!

* Don't hide any food in your bed(s) Squashed sausage-roll stains can be very hard to shift!

* Do dust the crumbs out of your bed before you settle down for the night. Sleeping on crumbly sheets is little-known form of torture!

EIGHT

Groovy Games

Games help to get a party get moving, and generally keep it groovin'! This chapter is full of games you can play before bedtime. Most of them need a bit of preparation and plenty of room to be played in.

Treasure Hunt

Can be played indoors and out of doors. Split everyone up into two teams of treasure hunters – that way everyone wins a prize.

You need two differently-coloured sheets of A4 paper so that each team knows which is theirs and no treasure seeker accidentally takes the clue of another team. Write instructions all the way across the back of each sheet about where the treasure is hidden, for example: 'Your goodies are stashed away in the washing machine.'

Next, cut up the piece of paper into ten small slips, and write a clue on the clean side of each slip. Keep the clues nice and puzzling, but make sure that your guests can easily find the objects you've chosen to hide clues under. (Remember that they won't know the layout of your house as well as you do, so stick to the kind of objects you'd find in most houses.)

These are a few good hiding places and clues:

"It's good to talk!"
– under the phone.
"It likes to be walked all over!"
– under your doormat.
"It's a window on the world."
– on your TV.
"It's not a board but you use it for surfing." – by the TV remote control.

When a team has collected all ten clues they can piece them together to reveal the message on the back of the sheet of paper and race to the treasure!

Who Am I?

You'll need:
- small pieces of paper and some felt tip pens
- safety pins

Each guest sits in a circle and writes down the name of a famous person on her slip of paper. She must then pin it to the back of her neighbour without her reading it. Choose names of pop stars, children's TV presenters, characters from fairy stories and nursery rhymes or famous sports personalities.

Each player must do a twirl to show everyone else who she's supposed to be. The aim of the game is to guess who you are by asking questions such as, 'Am I alive?' or, 'Am I a TV star?' The only answers are 'Yes' or 'No'. The person who asks the fewest questions to work out who they are is the winner.

Spin the Bottle

You'll need:

 a pointy bottle – an empty mineral-water bottle will do

 some fab forfeits

Everyone sits in a circle and takes turns at spinning the bottle. When the bottle stops, the person it is pointing at must take a truth or dare. They must answer a question truthfully (the more embarrassing the better!) or do a forfeit, for example, stand on their head or impersonate Cilla Black. Think up as many silly forfeits as you can before the game begins.

Taste Test

You'll need:

♈ blindfolds

♈ a selection of cups containing different (edible!) liquids

♈ teaspoons

Sit your guests around a table and blindfold them. Spoon a selection of drinks into their mouths. These might include tea, cola, fizzy mineral water, apple juice, cold gravy, salty water, etc. The person to make the most correct guesses about what they're tasting is the winner.

Guess the Gruesome Object

You'll need:

❓ blindfolds
❓ 'gruesome objects'

This is a brilliant game to play with lots of friends but you'll need to prepare it well before they arrive. The aim is to create a bowl (or bowls) of horrors to test their bravery. All they have to do is to sit in a circle, blindfolded. You then pass round a series of ghoulish objects, guaranteed to give them the willies. They have to work out what you're really handing them.

For example:

You say you're handing them . . .		When really you're giving them . . .
a plate of eyeballs	☞	peeled grapes in runny jelly
someone's tongue	☞	half a rasher of bacon
worms	☞	a handful of cold spaghetti

The first person to guess exactly what they're handling wins the point.

Murder in the Dark

You can play this game in your bedroom with the lights off, but it's even better if you take over the whole house.

You'll need:
- enough slips of paper for each player
- a pen

1   Mark one of the slips of paper with a cross and one with a circle. Then fold them all up and put them in a hat.

2   Ask each player to pick one. Whoever picks the circle is the detective and must identify herself straight away. Whoever picks the cross is the murderer and should keep quiet.

3   Turn off the lights and walk around the room (or house). Everyone except the murderer will be feeling pretty spooked – after all, they could be killed at any moment!

4 The murderer then selects her victim (it mustn't be the detective), approaches her, and taps her gently. The victim must then scream and fall to the floor. The murderer must try to get as far from the scene of the crime as possible. Once the scream is heard, the lights are turned on and the detective must try to work out who the murderer is.

5 In true whodunit style, the detective should question all the suspects to find out where they were when the murder happened. Only the murderer is allowed to lie, unless directly asked whether they are the killer. The detective gets just one go at guessing the murderer.

Make Your Own Video

If your family is lucky enough to own a video, you can perfect your Jeremy Beadle impression and capture your pyjama-drama on video. Here are a few tips to help make your video more interesting:

* Plan out what you're going to film before the party begins so that the video isn't too long and rambling.

* Give your friends star billing. Ask them to do a little speech to the camera.

* Aim to cover all the major events of the party. Include scenes you might think are boring such as eating tea and cleaning your teeth. In fact, they make for fascinating viewing!

* Make the pace fast and snappy. Don't spend too long filming any one scene.

* Instead of filming everything close up, how about a few shots from unusual angles. For example, you could film your guests arriving, perhaps from the top of the stairs or even from the outside of your house. (You may need another member of the family to help you film this scene.)

* Resist the temptation to watch your video until you wake up the next day!

Folklore Fun

Some people think that superstitions are silly but centuries ago, people lived their lives by them, wishing for luck, love, good health and wealth. Today much folklore has been forgotten. You probably know far fewer old wives tales and sayings than your great-grandmothers did. For example, finding a four-leafed clover is supposed to be lucky but do you know that finding a two-leafed clover means you'll soon get rich? And what's more, if two people eat a two-leafed clover together they will remain firm friends for ever. Quick, get combing the lawn!

These three old wives tales are supposed to give you a glimpse of your future love.

Peel an apple carefully so that the skin stays in one piece. Then lob the string of peel over your right shoulder. When it lands it should form the shape of your true love's initial. (You can do this little trick at any time of the year – but don't do it too often or you might end up with a whole alphabet of secret admirers!)

👁 On the first of May force yourself out of bed and into the garden just after sunrise while the ground's still damp. You should see the reflection of your true love in the dewy grass.

👁 Eat an apple on Hallow's Eve (that's 31 October – Halloween). Sit alone in front of a mirror by candle light, eating an apple. Close your eyes, then open them and you will see the face of your true love in the glass.

This old country spell is supposed to make you dream of your future husband.

Pick an ounce of St John's Wort and a handful of fresh rosemary at sunrise. Allow them to dry a little before sewing them into a small muslin bag. Then, place it underneath your pillow while repeating this spell:

St John, I pray have pity
In a vision let me see
My future husband to be
Scent of rosemary, opens hearts
Let me, my true love never part.

If you perform this spell properly, you never know, you might have visions of Ryan Giggs all night long.

St John's Wort is also known as Goatsweed or Amber. It has yellow flowers between June and September.

Top Party Tricks

There's nothing like a bit of magic to keep you amused, especially if it's done well. Entertain your pals with these amazing tricks. Or better still, perfect them together and amaze your families in the morning.

Catch it if you can

1   Take a banknote. Dangle it downwards, holding it along one of its short sides.

2   Then ask a friend to position their hand around the note, about half-way down. Their fingers must not actually touch the note, but when you let the note drop, they should be ready to catch it before it hits the ground.

3   Sounds easy? You'll be surprised to find that virtually no one will be quick enough to catch the falling banknote.

Water Joke

Fill a glass with water and leave it on a table. Tell everyone that you're going to leave the room but that before you walk back in again, the glass will be empty even though no one else will have touched it! How will this happen?

Walk out of the room and crawl back in again. Reach for the glass and guzzle the water down. Crawl out of the room and *now* walk in again.

Match Stick Magic

1   Hand your friends a box of matches and ask
them to pick one out and hand it to you. Get
them to nick it with a fingernail so that they'll
be able to recognize it later.

2   Next place the match in the centre of a hanky
and fold the cloth over it. Hold the
folded hanky out to your friends
and get one of them to feel
that the match is still
there. Ask them to
break the match
in half through
the cloth.

3 Open the handkerchief to reveal the match still in one piece and hand it back to the crowd!

How's it done? Before you do the trick, you have to sew a match into the hem of your hanky. Make sure this is the match that your friend feels and breaks when you hold it out to her.

Top Tip
It's best to put the hanky back in your pocket as soon as you've handed back the original match. Keep a second hanky ready in your pocket, just in case anyone asks to examine it to see how you did the trick.

Sugar Me!

1 Set up a bowl of sugar lumps on a table near you and take a lump of sugar in each hand, holding each one between a forefinger and thumb.

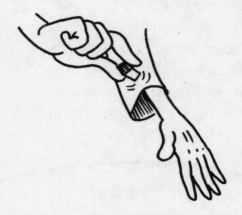

2 Rub one lump lightly against your sleeve, saying you will stick the two sugar lumps together with static electricity. Then press them together and they will miraculously stick.

3 Pop the two sugar lumps into your mouth. Then offer the bowl to your friends and ask them to try the trick too. They won't have any luck!

How's it done? Before you do the trick, you must rub a little butter onto one side of one of the sugar lumps you plan to use – the butter will glue the lumps together. Then put it back into the bowl. Make sure you pick the buttered lump when you start the trick.

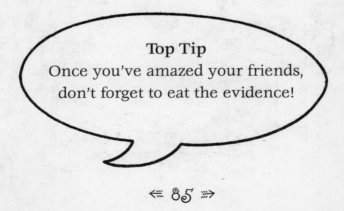

Top Tip
Once you've amazed your friends,
don't forget to eat the evidence!

NINE

Sleep-over Make over

Sleep-over parties are the perfect opportunity for you and your pals to pamper yourselves. Trying out a new look is ten times the fun with a chum to help, and you'll get a full and frank opinion as to whether it suits you when you're finished! Yes, sleep-over parties are the time to treat each other to relaxing and refreshing beauty treatments as well as an opportunity to exchange beauty tips and secrets.

You could start off with this recipe for hand lotion.

Lemon Hand Lotion

You will need:
Glycerine (you can buy this from a chemist)
Lemon juice
Eau de cologne (raid the bathroom cabinet!)

Mix two tablespoons each of lemon juice, glycerine
and eau de cologne to make a lovely hand lotion.
The lemon juice helps to keep your hands soft and
smooth and stops your nails from breaking.

Top Tip
Lemon juice
applied on a pad
of cotton wool is
a great toner for
oily skins.

Face Masks

Treat yourself to a facial and slap on a beauty mask to deep cleanse and liven up your skin. You simply put the mask on your face and leave it to set (but no laughing or it'll crack!) Then you rinse it off and feel totally facially freshed!

You can buy face masks from a shop, or, better still, raid the kitchen cupboard and make your own. Yes, though you might not realise it, many foods are full of cruelty-free beauty ingredients. Apples for example, are famous for their properties as a skin 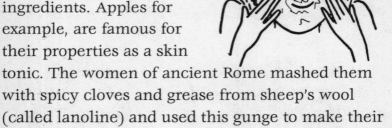 tonic. The women of ancient Rome mashed them with spicy cloves and grease from sheep's wool (called lanoline) and used this gunge to make their skin look great!

Before you choose a mask, it helps to know what kind of skin you've got.

Top Tip
After you've rinsed off a face mask, always splash your face with cold water to leave your skin glowing!

How do you know . . .

. . . if you've got oily skin?
Gently press a tissue over
your face first thing in the
morning. If it leaves an oily
mark, you've got oily skin.

. . . or dry skin?
If your skin feels tight in the
morning and/or has flaky
patches, it needs plenty of
moisturiser. Dry skin gets red
and sore in cold weather.

. . . or combination skin?
Actually most people have a
combination skin – oily patches
across the forehead and down
the middle of the face and
dryness on the cheeks.

. . . or sensitive skin?
Sensitive skins react to soap or
perfumes. They might come
up in a rash or inflamed patches
which can be sore or itchy.

Masks for Oily Skin

Green apple mask
Grate a green apple and spread it all over your face.
Wash off after ten minutes for firmer, fresher skin.

Egg white mask
Spread a raw egg white
thinly over your face
and leave it to set.
When the mask feels
tight and flaky, rinse it
off with warm water.

Honey mask

Spread a thin layer of honey over the face. Leave for about 15 minutes, then rinse off with hot water.

Deep-cleansing lemon mask

Add a little milk and lemon juice to a handful of oatmeal (natural bran or even Quick Quaker Oats will do) to make a paste.

Masks for Dry Skin

Avocado mask

Mash a ripe avocado with one teaspoonful of lemon juice and the white of an egg. When the mixture is smooth and soft, spread it over your face and leave for 20 minutes.

Strawberry cream mask

Mix a little fresh double cream and some fresh strawberries into a pulp. Spread over your face and leave for 15 minutes. Then rinse off with warm water.

Honey and egg mask

Take half a teaspoon of honey, one egg yolk and one tablespoon of dry skimmed milk powder. Mix to a paste (use a little fresh milk if necessary) and dab onto your face. Leave for 10 minutes and rinse off with warm water.

Warning: Take care to avoid your eyes when spreading a mask mixture onto your face. If you do get any of the mixture in your eyes, rinse it off at once with luke warm water.

Playing Footsie

If you've been running round all after-noon, evening is the right time to treat each other to a relaxing foot massage. It's easy to do – just follow the steps on the next page.

You'll need:

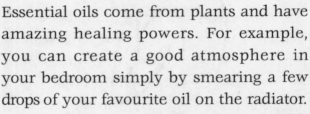

- Almond oil (a small bottle costs about a pound from your local chemist)
- Essential oils

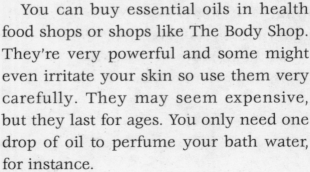

Essential oils come from plants and have amazing healing powers. For example, you can create a good atmosphere in your bedroom simply by smearing a few drops of your favourite oil on the radiator.

You can buy essential oils in health food shops or shops like The Body Shop. They're very powerful and some might even irritate your skin so use them very carefully. They may seem expensive, but they last for ages. You only need one drop of oil to perfume your bath water, for instance.

These three oils are safe for anyone to use and smell simply delicious:

Lavender Keeps you chilled out. If a friend has trouble sleeping, put a drop of lavender on her pilow.

Geranium Also good for relaxing. Geranium gets rid of pre-PJ party nerves and will help make your pals feel at home.

Rose Although it's incredibly expensive in it's purest form, just a whiff of this oil can lift your spirits if you're feeling a bit down! The good news is that you can also buy rose oil diluted in jojoba oil, which is much cheaper but still does the business! Roman Emperors were so fond of the smell that they poured rose water into the canals running through their gardens. Add a few drops of rose oil to the final rinse of your hair and it will smell magic.

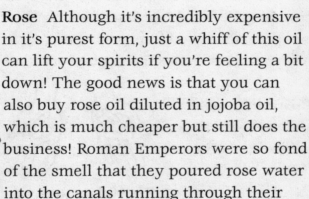

How to Master a
Basic Foot Massage

1   Ask your friend to lie down on the floor. Sit cross-legged, facing her. Spread a towel over your lap (this will stop oil from getting on the carpet). Ask your friend to rest her foot on your knee.

2   Take a handful of oil and mix with a drop of essential oil.

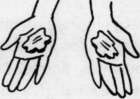

3   Hold your friend's foot steady with one hand. Massage the foot with the other.

4   Make your hand into a fist and make small circle movements along the sole of the foot. Press hard.

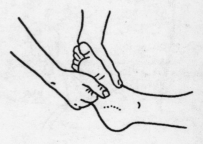

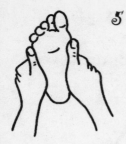

5 Next, press the sole of the foot with both your thumbs. (You'll have to hold the foot steady with your fingers for this one.) Go over every bit of the sole pressing quite hard.

6 Using your thumbs again, press over the top of the foot (i.e. the other side).

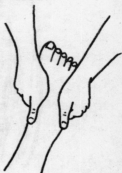

7 To finish off, gently squeeze the foot all over.

Top Tips
If you haven't any oil, talcum powder will do. But don't add any essential oil to it or you'll end up with a pongy goo!

Eye Pick-me-ups

Try these three 10-minute treats for tired eyes.

👁 Thinly slice a cucumber and layer the slices over your eyelids until your whole eye area is completely covered.

👁 Put slices of raw potato over your eyes to soothe headaches, make your eyelids less puffy and refresh tired eyes.

👁 Pop a cold tea bag on each eye, lie back and let this tea-licious brew pep up your peepers.

Bath Time Bliss

Add one drop of geranium oil and one drop of orange oil for a fruitfully refreshing bath.

Or

Add one drop of lavender oil and one drop of camomile German for a kind of blissed-out bubble gum aroma.

Hair Styles

Here are some brilliant ways to work that hair. Lots of these styles are particularly good for overnight parties since you need a patient helper to perfect the style and do the tricky bits at the back.

We've given them a difficulty rating as follows:

★★★★★   dead easy
★★★★   easy
★★★   quite hard
★★   put in a little practice
★   you've been warned!

My little ponies

Make two small high bunches of hair from the back of the head near the crown, leaving the rest of the hair loose. Secure the bunches with stretchy bands. Add ribbons for that finishing touch!
★★★★★

Funky frizz

Wet your hair, divide into lots of thin sections and plait all over. Tie off each plait with cotton thread to stop it coming undone. Make two tiny fine plaits at the front and thread with beads.
Pull out a little hair from the plait just below the beads to keep them in place. Leave your hair to dry overnight. Then undo all except the front plaits and your hair will frizz! ★★★

Do the twist

Part your hair into thin
strands. Twist each
strand until it starts
buckling. Keep twisting,
so the hair keeps
buckling, until you
can't twist any more.
Then pin down the loose ends of the hair section
with a hair grip. ★★★★★

Beehive

Sport a beehive for that
fab fifties look. Backcomb
your hair (literally comb
it backwards with a fine
comb instead of for-
wards).When your hair
becomes stiff and bushy,
brush it to one side, turn
the hair in on itself and
pin with grips. Work your
way up the back of your head, creating as much
bulk on top as possible for a big beehive, sweetie!
Hair spray will help to stiffen your hair and
hold it up. ★

Natty dreads

Tie your hair in a high ponytail on top of your head. It's best if you bend over and let your hair fall right over your face as you do this. Make sure the pony tail is nice and tight, and then comb the hair and separate it into tiny strands. Plait these strands and tie them with embroidery silks or cotton thread so they can't come undone, and hey presto, instant dreads! ✦✦✦✦

Best Bunches

Part your hair into two even bunches. Then evenly space brightly coloured stretchy hair bands down the length of the bunches. Simple but very effective.
✦✦✦✦✦

Top Tip
It's easier to plait your hair
if it's wet.

TEN

Pillow Talk

Ker-lick! The laughs don't have to stop when the lights go out. There are lots of hilarious games to play after dark, quite apart from the chance to catch up with some serious pillow talk.

Getting Wordy

Word games are especially fun to play in the dark where there are no other distractions. You're forced to really listen to what everyone's saying (unless you fall asleep first). Inventing new words is a great pillow game – make up some new swear words such as 'Flubberbucket' and 'Brummocks'! They'll tickle you pink, and your mum and dad won't even realize you're being naughty next time you need to let off steam.

Other fun word games include:

- ○ Making up new weird and wonderful flavours for crisps (such as fried egg and bacon, and mouldy cheese and onion).

- ○ Inventing new exotic perfume flavours (such as Scent of Garlic Bread, Banana Daquiri, or Pammy for Men!).

Tongue Twisters

Get your tangue all tongled up saying these silly sentences as fast as you can.

"Red lorry, yellow lorry."
"The sun shines on shop signs."
"She sells sea-shells by the sea shore."
"The cruel ghoul's cool gruel."

Now have a go at inventing your own.

How do you know when someone's sleeping like a log?
You can hear them sawing!

Lottery Fever!

This is a game to test
the powers of your
imagination. It
also gives you
the chance of
indulging in your favourite fantasy . . .
working out what'll you do with
all that cash if you strike it lucky
on the lottery.

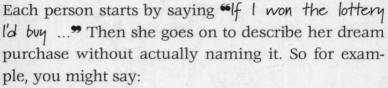

Each person starts by saying "If I won the lottery I'd buy ..." Then she goes on to describe her dream purchase without actually naming it. So for example, you might say:

"I'd buy a famous building in London, where people sit down to scoff. It's full of very valuable objects that have appeared in famous films. It's owned by three mega movie stars."

Anyone can interrupt as soon as they know what you're talking about. (Can you guess where the example is? . . . Planet Hollywood.)

Keep your clues vague, but accurate and fair. Pause after each description to see if anyone can guess what it is, and carry on if nobody gets it right.

What Happened Next?

In this storytelling game each player takes a turn at unfolding the tale. One person starts the story – and since you'll be playing this in the dark, it ought to be a ghost story! When she reaches a really exciting or scarey bit, the narrator stops, and the next person takes up the story, and so on. You can keep playing this game until either you drift off to sleep or spook yourselves silly!

What knocks you out every night, but can't harm you?
Sleep!

Me and My Shadow

If you've got a torch, make shadow shapes against the wall. Put your torch on a table or chair so that it shines onto the wall. Hold your arms and hands in the beam of light so that it casts a shadow onto the wall.

Copy these simple shapes, though you can experiment too, and make up lots more for yourself.

cat

swan

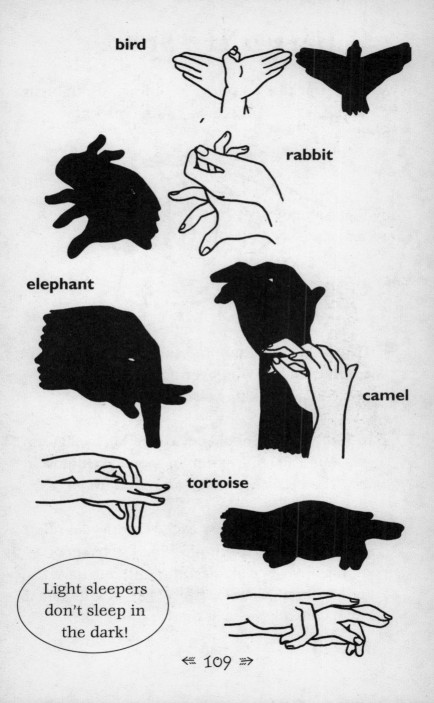

bird

rabbit

elephant

camel

tortoise

Light sleepers don't sleep in the dark!

Here is the Snooze

We interrupt this chapter on pillow talk to bring you some fascinating facts you never knew about sleep!

👁 Three-toed sloths are the sleepiest mammals around. They spend over nineteen out of every 24 hours a day a-snoozing!

👁 In 1987, an 11-year-old boy called Michael Dixon was found 100 miles from his home in Illinois in the USA after sleepwalking onto a train!

👁 Victims of a rare illness called chronic colestites suffer from total insomnia which stops them getting any sleep at all. Some sufferers have gone without sleep for five years – it's enough to make you fall asleep at the very thought!

👁 The record-breaking, ear-bursting snores of Kare Walkert of Kumala, Sweden, were measured while he kipped in hospital on 24 May 1993. Kare suffers from a breathing disorder called apnea, and his sleepy sounds peaked at a whopping 93 decibels. That's louder than a pneumatic drill in heavy traffic!

👁 If you don't get enough sleep you can go quite mad! People who are deprived of sleep become cross, clumsy and forgetful. They may start seeing things and can even go crazy. Depriving someone from sleeping has been used as a particularly cruel form of torture.

Three famous people who thrived on very little sleep: Thomas Edison, Napoleon Bonaparte, Margaret Thatcher!

What do you call an outdoor sleep-over?
In-tents entertainment

👁 Sugar can make you sleepy. Eating sweets creates more of a special chemical in your brain that calms down brain actvity, making you feel relaxed and sleepy.

👁 Contrary to popular belief, a glass of milk at bedtime won't help you to drift off into the land of nod. Milk (at least skimmed or low-fat milk) actually perks up brain chemicals making it harder to fall asleep.

👁 REM isn't just the name of a top rock band. In science it's the dreaming stage of sleep during which a person's eyes dart around under the eyelids. REM stands for rapid-eye-movement sleep and it usually occurs just after you've nodded off, or just before you wake up.

👁 Sometimes you can be woken from REM sleep easily, at other times it's very difficult. An alarm clock radio may not wake you immediately from a really interesting dream. Instead, you might include something you hear on the radio in your dream. So if you find yourself dreaming about Chris Evans, you'll know why!

To which question can you never answer 'Yes'?
'Are you asleep?'

Secret Confessions

Now, back to your bedroom. It's time for some true confessions. Swapping secrets can be fun, especially if you've been dying to get something off your chest for ages. But you might want to bear a few points in mind. When you're cosy and warm and on the verge of falling asleep, you could easily say something you'll regret the next day. So remember:

❤ Don't tell a friend anything you really want to be a secret. It's too much to expect even your bestest buddy to keep a really juicy secret to themselves for ever!

❤ Never make anything up. If your mate finds out you've been telling porky pies she might feel hurt.

❤ A real friend never forces another person to reveal her innermost thoughts.

Boyz Talk

When girls get together with their mates you can guarantee that at some point boys are going to be discussed.

Three things you should know about boys:

❤ They are strangely terrified of girls and yet have no fear of slugs, stick insects and other creepy crawlies.

❤ Even though they might like you very much, they will only be nice to you when their friends aren't looking.

❤ Don't expect boys to waste time talking about girls at *their* sleep-overs. They're far too busy playing practical tricks on their parents, scoffing midnight feasts, flashing their torches, shooting their super-soaker guns out of the window and playing pogs.

Boys are a truly fascinating species – but however interesting they are to talk about, you will find, sooner or later, that you still eventually drop off to sleep . . .

Sweet Dreams

We all dream every night during REM sleep (though some of us think we don't because we simply can't remember our dreams). Dreams are fascinating things. They can give us ideas for stories, for instance. Some people believe that dreams can even predict the future or are a way of telling us what we want from life – our subconscious thoughts.

These are a few of the commonest dreams, and what they are supposed to mean.

Teeth
Dreaming that your teeth are falling out means that your life is just about to change.

Money
Dreaming of finding or spending money usually means that money worries are on the way. Be extra careful with your pocket money.

Exams

Lots of people dream about taking exams, especially when they're revising for one. It's usually a sign that you're a bit anxious but then who wouldn't be? Dreaming that you've failed an exam means that you should think carefully about something which is bugging you.

Flying

Dreaming of flying means that you're a bit of an escapist. You feel unworthy and can't imagine that your ambitions will ever be fulfilled. You're just crying out to be noticed – by flying you're showing others just how clever you really are.

Hiding

To dream that you're hiding means that you're frightened your secrets will be revealed.

The Morning After

Dust the crumbs out of your duvet and roll up that sleeping bag. It's morning and it will soon be time to say goodbye to your friends. Sob! Even so, you can still make the most of the morning.

🕐 Set your alarm clock for sevenish. You may be on such a party-high that you won't need it, especially if you're an early riser anyway. But if you stayed up talking or feasting all night you could easily oversleep. Remember, now is not the time for snoozing. Now is the time for a bit more partying!

🕐 Drag yourselves up and tip toe down to your kitchen to make brekkie. (How about coco pops with chopped banana, and jam and marshmallow spread on toast?) But a word of warning – don't bother to treat your parents to a trayful. Parents get dead grumpy if they're woken before nine at weekends!

🕐 Once you've had your fill of early-morning fodder, drag your duvets down from your bedroom and settle on the sofa for an hour or two with your favourite video. Smart hosts save the best video for now. But another warning – keep the volume down until after nine (for reasons already mentioned!).

🕐 If you're making a video of your pyjama party, don't forget to capture breakfast on camera! Early morning is the ideal time to rewind the tape and relive the party's finest moments.

🕐 Once Mum and Dad are up, you won't have to worry about keeping the noise down so much and you'll have the run of the house again. Depending on what time the party is set to end, you could get a few more games in. You might want to stage another treasure hunt now – perhaps you could hide going-home presents for your guests. They won't be able to leave without them!

Good Guests Always . . .

★ Make sure they are awake by the time their parents come to collect them.

★ Have a good rummage around the house to make sure they haven't left any clobber behind.

★ Remember to thank their host for such a fun time.

Good Hosts Always . . .

* Arrange an early morning alarm call if there's any chance of oversleeping.

* Double-check that their guests haven't left any clobber behind.

* Remember to thank their guests for being such fun!

And whether you're a host or a guest . . .

* when the party is over you could find yourself feeling a little glum without your chums. Cheer yourself up by planning a return party in the near future.

  Warning: if you had a particularly fun time, leave it at least a week before organizing a follow-up. Your parents will thank you for it!

TWELVE

Sleep-over in the Strangest of Places

Once you've mastered a sleep-over at home, how about a sleep-over in a museum or your local library? You could even organize a sponsored sleep-out in a church hall or castle.

Museums

More and more museums are hosting slumber parties, giving you the chance to stay among the exhibits and take part in an evening of activities.

Most museums open their doors between 6.30p.m. and 7.00p.m. Slumberers are usually welcomed in largish groups with at least one adult to supervise. However, some places provide child minders.

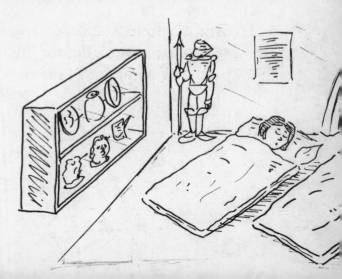

- The Science Museum, London hosts a sleep-over party every month (except August). The parties are called Science Nights, and they cater for a maximum of 380 eight- to eleven-year-olds, plus about 80 accompanying adults. These evenings are extremely popular so book early!

  All children must come as part of a group, of between six and nine kids. And all groups must be accompanied by up to two adults. Call the Science Museum on 0171 938 9785.

- The Royal Museum of Scotland, Edinburgh held a slumber party to celebrate Science Week in 1996. Over 150 eight- to eleven-year-olds were invited. The sleep-over was such a success that the Science Festival is considering hosting more pyjama parties in the future. Contact the Science Festival office on 0131 220 6220.

 The National Railway Museum, York hosts
Night Train, a twice yearly sleep-over where up
to 200 children and parents can join in the fun.
There must be one adult for every five children.

    The evening kicks off at approximately
6.30p.m. with a tour of the museum, before
guests are invited to take part in games and
craft workshops. There's a ghost story-telling
session and even a midnight feast. The fun
doesn't finish there. At 8.00a.m. the next
morning, you'll be served a well-deserved
breakfast! Call the National Railway Museum
on 01904 621261.

     Techniquest in Cardiff used to host regular
sleep-overs before it moved to new premises.
Unfortunately, the new building isn't perfect
for pjyama parties but we're told that plans
are afoot to convert it so that Science Nights
can start up again soon. Telephone 01222 475475.

The National Museum of Photography, Film and Television in Bradford holds two or three Camps-Ins a year. Each Camp-In is themed. Guests watch cartoons in the museum's cinema.

Then there are projects and a midnight feast. Whilst the visitors sleep the staff work editing the videos, ready to be shown after breakfast.Call the National Museum of Photography, Film and Television on 01274 727488.

Eureka! in Halifax has hosted sleep-overs in the past and plans to host more in the future.Call Eureka! on 01422 330069.

Many libraries also host sleep-overs – they're the perfect place for a top night of story-telling. Call your central libraries office for details.

In-tents Excitement!

In 1907 the founder of the Scouting and Guiding movement, Robert Baden-Powell held an experimental camp on Brownsea Island in Dorset. Ever since, camps and pack holidays have remained an important and well-loved part of Scouting and Guiding.

If you fancy a night or two away with your pack, fending for yourself and your friends, then Guide camp could be for you. Don't expect to be surrounded by home comforts – you're more likely to be collecting firewood or enjoying a torch-lit ramble than watching French and Saunders on video! Brownie and Guiding holidays are packed with activities and challenges designed to build your confidence and increase skills that help you in everyday life. Camp is also a great way to bond with your buddies.

If you're a Brownie (aged 7–10) you can go on pack holidays for one or two nights indoors or under canvas. But Brownie Guides must be at least nine years old to go to Guide camp. Ask your leader for more details. To find out more about being in the Brownies/Guides write to The Guide Association, 17–19 Buckingham Palace Road, London SW1W 0PT. Tel: 0171 834 6242.

Although a Guide camp or a museum pyjama party can be great fun, you don't need a special place or even lots of guests to have a fantastic sleep-over. Just one friend visiting for the night can make for a great time. All you need is to plan carefully, take good care of your guests and, above all, have fun! Happy sleep-overs!